'She has many rare and charming qualities, but Sobriety is not one of them . . .'

JANE AUSTEN
Born 1775, Hampshire, England
Died 1817, Hampshire, England

Selected from *Love and Freindship and Other Youthful Writings*,
edited by Christine Alexander.

AUSTEN IN PENGUIN CLASSICS
Love and Freindship and Other Youthful Writings
Northanger Abbey
Sense and Sensibility
Pride and Prejudice
Mansfield Park
Emma
Persuasion
Lady Susan / The Watsons / Sanditon

JANE AUSTEN

The Beautifull Cassandra

PENGUIN BOOKS

PENGUIN CLASSICS

Published by the Penguin Group
Penguin Books Ltd, 80 Strand, London WC2R ORL, England
Penguin Group (USA) Inc., 375 Hudson Street, New York, New York 10014, USA
Penguin Group (Canada), 90 Eglinton Avenue East, Suite 700, Toronto, Ontario,
Canada M4P 2Y3 (a division of Pearson Penguin Canada Inc.)
Penguin Ireland, 25 St Stephen's Green, Dublin 2, Ireland
(a division of Penguin Books Ltd)
Penguin Group (Australia), 707 Collins Street, Melbourne, Victoria 3008, Australia
(a division of Pearson Australia Group Pty Ltd)
Penguin Books India Pvt Ltd, 11 Community Centre, Panchsheel Park,
New Delhi – 110 017, India
Penguin Group (NZ), 67 Apollo Drive, Rosedale, Auckland 0632, New Zealand
(a division of Pearson New Zealand Ltd)
Penguin Books (South Africa) (Pty) Ltd, Block D, Rosebank Office Park,
181 Jan Smuts Avenue, Parktown North, Gauteng 2193, South Africa

Penguin Books Ltd, Registered Offices: 80 Strand, London WC2R ORL, England

www.penguin.com

This selection published in Penguin Classics 2015
002

Set in 9.5/13 pt Baskerville 10 Pro
Typeset by Jouve (UK), Milton Keynes
Printed in Great Britain by Clays Ltd, St Ives plc

A CIP catalogue record for this book is available from the British Library

ISBN: 978–0–141–39707–8

www.greenpenguin.co.uk

MIX
Paper from
responsible sources
FSC www.fsc.org FSC™ C018179

Penguin Books is committed to a sustainable
future for our business, our readers and our planet.
This book is made from Forest Stewardship
Council™ certified paper.

Contents

Jack and Alice

a novel

Is respectfully inscribed to Francis William Austen Esqr Midshipman on board his Majesty's Ship the Perseverance

by his obedient humble

Servant The Author

CHAPTER THE FIRST

Mr Johnson was once upon a time about 53; in a twelve-month afterwards he was 54, which so much delighted him that he was determined to celebrate his next Birth day by giving a Masquerade to his Children and Freinds. Accordingly on the Day he attained his 55th year tickets were dispatched to all his Neighbours to that purpose. His acquaintance indeed in that part of the World were not very numerous as they consisted only of Lady Williams, M^r and Mrs Jones, Charles Adams and the 3 Miss Simpsons, who composed the neighbourhood of Pammydiddle and formed the Masquerade.

Before I proceed to give an account of the Evening, it

will be proper to describe to my reader, the persons and Characters of the party introduced to his acquaintance.

M^r and Mrs Jones were both rather tall and very passionate, but were in other respects, good tempered, wellbehaved People. Charles Adams was an amiable, accomplished and bewitching young Man; of so dazzling a Beauty that none but Eagles could look him in the Face.

Miss Simpson was pleasing in her person, in her Manners and in her Disposition; an unbounded ambition was her only fault. Her second sister Sukey was Envious, Spitefull and Malicious. Her person was short, fat and disagreable. Cecilia (the youngest) was perfectly handsome but too affected to be pleasing.

In Lady Williams every virtue met. She was a widow with a handsome Jointure and the remains of a very handsome face. Tho' Benevolent and Candid, she was Generous and sincere; Tho' Pious and Good, she was Religious and amiable, and Tho' Elegant and Agreable, she was Polished and Entertaining.

The Johnsons were a family of Love, and though a little addicted to the Bottle and the Dice, had many good Qualities.

Such was the party assembled in the elegant Drawing Room of Johnson Court, amongst which the pleasing figure of a Sultana was the most remarkable of the female Masks. Of the Males a Mask representing the Sun, was the most universally admired. The Beams that darted from his Eyes were like those of that glorious Luminary tho' infinitely superior. So strong were they that no one dared venture within half a mile of them; he had therefore the best part of the Room to himself, its size not amounting to more than 3 quarters of a mile in length and half a one in breadth. The Gentleman at last finding the feirceness of his beams to be very inconvenient to the concourse by obliging them to croud together in one corner of the room, half shut his eyes by which means, the Company discovered him to be Charles Adams in his plain green Coat, without any mask at all.

When their astonishment was a little subsided their attention was attracted by 2 Dominos who advanced in a horrible Passion; they were both very tall, but seemed in other respects to have many good qualities. 'These,' said the witty Charles, 'these are M^r and Mrs Jones,' and so indeed they were.

No one could imagine who was the Sultana! Till at length on her addressing a beautifull Flora who was reclining in a studied attitude on a couch, with 'Oh Cecilia, I wish I was really what I pretend to be', she was discovered by the never failing genius of Charles Adams, to be the elegant but ambitious Caroline Simpson, and the person to whom she addressed herself, he rightly imagined to be her lovely but affected sister Cecilia.

The Company now advanced to a Gaming Table where sat 3 Dominos (each with a bottle in their hand) deeply engaged; but a female in the character of Virtue fled with hasty footsteps from the shocking scene, whilst a little fat woman representing Envy, sate alternately on the foreheads of the 3 Gamesters. Charles Adams was still as bright as ever; he soon discovered the party at play to be the 3 Johnsons, Envy to be Sukey Simpson and Virtue to be Lady Williams.

The Masks were then all removed and the Company retired to another room, to partake of an elegant and well managed Entertainment, after which the Bottle being pretty briskly pushed about by the 3 Johnsons, the whole party not excepting even Virtue were carried home, Dead Drunk.

CHAPTER THE SECOND

For three months did the Masquerade afford ample subject for conversation to the inhabitants of Pammydiddle; but no character at it was so fully expatiated on as Charles Adams. The singularity of his appearance, the beams which darted from his eyes, the brightness of his Wit, and the whole <u>tout ensemble</u> of his person had subdued the hearts of so many of the young Ladies, that of the six present at the Masquerade but five had returned uncaptivated. Alice Johnson was the unhappy sixth whose heart had not been able to withstand the power of his Charms. But as it may appear strange to my Readers, that so much worth and Excellence as he possessed should have conquered only hers, it will be necessary to inform them that the Miss Simpsons were defended from his Power by Ambition, Envy, and Selfadmiration.

Every wish of Caroline was centered in a titled Husband; whilst in Sukey such superior excellence could only raise her Envy not her Love, and Cecilia was too tenderly attached to herself to be pleased with any one besides. As for Lady Williams and Mrs Jones, the former of them was too sensible, to fall in love with one so much her Junior and the latter, tho' very tall and very passionate was too fond of her Husband to think of such a thing.

Yet in spite of every endeavour on the part of Miss Johnson to discover any attachment to her in him; the cold and indifferent heart of Charles Adams still to all appearance, preserved its native freedom; polite to all but partial to none, he still remained the lovely, the lively, but insensible Charles Adams.

One evening, Alice finding herself somewhat heated by wine (no very uncommon case) determined to seek a releif for her disordered Head and Love-sick Heart in the Conversation of the intelligent Lady Williams.

She found her Ladyship at home as was in general the Case, for she was not fond of going out, and like the great Sir Charles Grandison scorned to deny herself when at Home, as she looked on that fashionable method of shutting out disagreable Visitors, as little less than downright Bigamy.

In spite of the wine she had been drinking, poor Alice was uncommonly out of spirits; she could think of nothing but Charles Adams, she could talk of nothing but him, and in short spoke so openly that Lady Williams soon discovered the unreturned affection she bore him, which excited her Pity and Compassion so strongly that she addressed her in the following Manner.

'I perceive but too plainly my dear Miss Johnson, that your Heart has not been able to withstand the fascinating Charms of this Young Man and I pity you sincerely. Is it a first Love?'

'It is.'

'I am still more greived to hear <u>that</u>; I am myself a sad example of the Miseries, in general attendant on a first Love and I am determined for the future to avoid the like Misfortune. I wish it may not be too late for you to do the same; if it is not endeavour my dear Girl to secure yourself from so great a Danger. A second attachment is seldom attended with any serious consequences; against <u>that</u> therefore I have nothing to say. Preserve yourself from a first Love and you need not fear a second.'

'You mentioned Madam something of your having yourself been a sufferer by the misfortune you are so good as to wish me to avoid. Will you favour me with your Life and Adventures?'

'Willingly my Love.'

CHAPTER THE THIRD

'My Father was a gentleman of considerable Fortune in Berkshire; myself and a few more his only Children. I was but six years old when I had the misfortune of losing my Mother and being at that time young and Tender, my father instead of sending me to School, procured an able handed Governess to superintend my Education at Home. My Brothers were placed at Schools suitable to their Ages and my Sisters being all younger than myself, remained still under the Care of their Nurse.

'Miss Dickins was an excellent Governess. She instructed me in the Paths of Virtue; under her tuition I daily became more amiable, and might perhaps by this time have nearly attained perfection, had not my worthy Preceptoress been torn from my arms, e'er I had attained my seventeenth year. I never shall forget her last words. "My dear Kitty" she said. "Good night t'ye." I never saw her afterwards,' continued Lady Williams wiping her eyes, 'She eloped with the Butler the same night.

'I was invited the following year by a distant relation of my Father's to spend the Winter with her in town. Mrs Watkins was a Lady of Fashion, Family and fortune; she was in general esteemed a pretty Woman, but I never thought her very handsome, for my part. She had too high a forehead, Her eyes were too small and she had too much colour.'

'How can <u>that</u> be?' interrupted Miss Johnson reddening with anger; 'Do you think that any one can have too much colour?'

'Indeed I do, and I'll tell you why I do my dear Alice; when a person has too great a degree of red in their Complexion, it gives their face in my opinion, too red a look.'

'But can a face my Lady have too red a look?'

'Certainly my dear Miss Johnson and I'll [tell] you why. When a face has too red a look it does not appear to so much advantage as it would were it paler.'

'Pray Ma'am proceed in your story.'

'Well, as I said before, I was invited by this Lady to spend some weeks with her in town. Many Gentlemen thought her Handsome but in my opinion, Her forehead was too high, her eyes too small and she had too much colour.'

'In that Madam as I said before your Ladyship must have been mistaken. Mrs Watkins could not have too much colour since no one can have too much.'

'Excuse me my Love if I do not agree with you in that particular. Let me explain myself clearly; my idea of the case is this. When a Woman has too great a proportion of red in her Cheeks, she must have too much colour.'

'But Madam I deny that it is possible for any one to have too great a proportion of red in their Cheeks.'

'What my Love not if they have too much colour?'

Miss Johnson was now out of all patience, the more so perhaps as Lady Williams still remained so inflexibly cool.

It must be remembered however that her Ladyship had in one respect by far the advantage of Alice; I mean in not being drunk, for heated with wine and raised by Passion, she could have little command of her Temper.

The Dispute at length grew so hot on the part of Alice that 'From Words she almost came to Blows' When Mr Johnson luckily entered and with some difficulty forced her away from Lady Williams, Mrs Watkins and her red cheeks.

CHAPTER THE FOURTH

My Readers may perhaps imagine that after such a fracas, no intimacy could longer subsist between the Johnsons and Lady Williams, but in that they are mistaken for her Ladyship was too sensible to be angry at a conduct which she could not help perceiving to be the natural consequence of inebriety and Alice had too sincere a respect for Lady Williams and too great a relish for her Claret, not to make every concession in her power.

A few days after their reconciliation Lady Williams called on Miss Johnson to propose a walk in a Citron Grove which led from her Ladyship's pigstye to Charles Adams's Horsepond. Alice was too sensible of Lady Williams's kindness in proposing such a walk and too much pleased with the prospect of seeing at the end of it, a Horsepond of Charles's, not to accept it with visible delight. They had not proceeded far before she was roused from the reflection of the happiness she was going to enjoy, by Lady Williams's thus addressing her.

'I have as yet forborn my dear Alice to continue the narrative of my Life from an unwillingness of recalling to your Memory a scene which (since it reflects on you rather disgrace than credit) had better be forgot than remembered.'

Alice had already begun to colour up and was beginning to speak, when her Ladyship perceiving her displeasure, continued thus.

'I am afraid my dear Girl that I have offended you by what I have just said; I assure you I do not mean to distress you by a retrospection of what cannot now be helped; considering all things I do not think you so much to blame as many People do; for when a person is in Liquor, there is no answering for what they may do.'

'Madam, this is not to be borne; I insist—'

'My dear Girl don't vex yourself about the matter; I assure you I have entirely forgiven every thing respecting it; indeed I was not angry at the time, because as I saw all along, you were nearly dead drunk. I knew you could not help saying the strange things you did. But I see I distress you; so I will change the subject and desire it may never again be mentioned; remember it is all forgot – I will now pursue my story; but I must insist upon not giving you any description of Mrs Watkins; it would only be reviving old stories and as you never saw her, it can be nothing to you, if her forehead <u>was</u> too high, her eyes <u>were</u> too small, or if she <u>had</u> too much colour.'

'Again! Lady Williams: this is too much—'

So provoked was poor Alice at this renewal of the old story, that I know not what might have been the consequence of it, had not their attention been engaged by another object. A lovely young Woman lying apparently in great pain beneath a Citron-tree, was an object too interesting not to attract their notice. Forgetting their own dispute they both with simpathizing Tenderness advanced towards her and accosted her in these terms.

'You seem fair Nymph to be labouring under some misfortune which we shall be happy to releive if you will inform us what it is. Will you favour us with your Life and adventures?'

'Willingly Ladies, if you will be so kind as to be seated.' They took their places and she thus began.

CHAPTER THE FIFTH

'I am a native of North Wales and my Father is one of the most capital Taylors in it. Having a numerous family, he was easily prevailed on by a sister of my Mother's who is a widow in good circumstances and keeps an alehouse in the next Village to ours, to let her take me and breed me up at her own expence. Accordingly I have lived with her for the last 8 years of my Life, during which time she provided me with some of the first rate Masters, who taught me all the accomplishments requisite for one of my sex and rank. Under their instructions I learned Dancing, Music, Drawing and various Languages, by which means I became more accomplished than any other Taylor's Daughter in Wales. Never was there a happier Creature than I was, till within the last half year – but I should have told you before that the principal Estate in our Neighbourhood belongs to Charles Adams, the owner of the brick House, you see yonder.'

'Charles Adams!' exclaimed the astonished Alice; 'are you acquainted with Charles Adams?'

'To my sorrow madam I am. He came about half a year ago to receive the rents of the Estate I have just mentioned. At that time I first saw him; as you seem ma'am acquainted with him, I need not describe to you how charming he is. I could not resist his attractions;—'

'Ah! who can,' said Alice with a deep sigh.

'My Aunt being in terms of the greatest intimacy with his cook, determined, at my request, to try whether she could discover, by means of her freind if there were any chance of his returning my affection. For this purpose she went one evening to drink tea with Mrs Susan, who in the course of Conversation mentioned the goodness of her Place and the Goodness of her Master; upon which my Aunt began pumping her with so much dexterity that in a short time Susan owned, that she did not think her Master would ever marry, "for (said she) he has often and often declared to me that his wife, whoever she might be, must possess, Youth, Beauty, Birth, Wit, Merit, and Money. I have many a time (she continued) endeavoured to reason him out of his resolution and to convince him of the improbability of his ever meeting with such a Lady; but my arguments have had no effect and he continues as firm in his determination as ever." You may imagine Ladies my distress on hearing this; for I was fearfull that tho' possessed of Youth, Beauty, Wit and Merit, and tho' the probable Heiress of my Aunts House and business, he might think me deficient in Rank, and in being so, unworthy of his hand.

'However I was determined to make a bold push and therefore wrote him a very kind letter, offering him with great tenderness my hand and heart. To this I received an angry and peremptory refusal, but thinking it might be rather the effect of his modesty than any thing else, I pressed him again on the subject. But he never answered any more of my Letters and very soon afterwards left the Country. As soon as I heard of his departure I wrote to him here, informing him that I should shortly do myself the honour of waiting on him at Pammydiddle, to which I received no answer; therefore choosing to take, Silence for Consent, I left Wales, unknown to my Aunt, and arrived here after a tedious Journey this Morning. On enquiring for his House I was directed thro' this Wood, to the one you there see. With a heart elated by the expected happiness of beholding him I entered it and

13

had proceeded thus far in my progress thro' it, when I found myself suddenly seized by the leg and on examining the cause of it, found that I was caught in one of the steel traps so common in gentlemen's grounds.'

'Ah,' cried Lady Williams, 'how fortunate we are to meet with you; since we might otherwise perhaps have shared the like misfortune—'

'It is indeed happy for you Ladies, that I should have been a short time before you. I screamed as you may easily imagine till the woods resounded again and till one of the inhuman Wretch's servants came to my assistance and released me from my dreadfull prison, but not before one of my legs was entirely broken.'

CHAPTER THE SIXTH

At this melancholy recital the fair eyes of Lady Williams, were suffused in tears and Alice could not help exclaiming,

'Oh! cruel Charles to wound the hearts and legs of all the fair.'

Lady Williams now interposed and observed that the young Lady's leg ought to be set without farther delay. After examining the fracture therefore, she immediately began and performed the operation with great skill which was the more wonderfull on account of her having never performed such a one before. Lucy, then arose from the ground and finding that she could walk with the greatest ease, accompanied them to Lady Williams's House at her Ladyship's particular request.

The perfect form, the beautifull face, and elegant manners of Lucy so won on the affections of Alice that when they parted, which was not till after Supper, she assured her that except her Father, Brother, Uncles, Aunts, Cousins and other relations, Lady Williams, Charles Adams and a few dozen more of particular freinds, she loved her better than almost any other person in the world.

Such a flattering assurance of her regard would justly have given much pleasure to the object of it, had she not plainly perceived that the amiable Alice had partaken too freely of Lady Williams's claret.

Her Ladyship (whose discernment was great) read in the intelligent countenance of Lucy her thoughts on the subject and as soon as Miss Johnson had taken her leave, thus addressed her.

'When you are more intimately acquainted with my Alice you will not be surprised, Lucy, to see the dear Creature drink a little too much; for such things happen every day. She has many rare and charming qualities, but Sobriety is not one of them. The whole Family are indeed a sad drunken set. I am sorry to say too that I never knew three such thorough Gamesters as they are, more particularly Alice. But she is a charming girl. I fancy not one of the sweetest tempers in the world; to be sure I have seen her in such passions! However she is a sweet young Woman. I am sure you'll like her. I scarcely know any one so amiable. – Oh! that you could but have seen her the other Evening! How she raved! and on such a trifle too! She is indeed a most pleasing Girl! I shall always love her!'

'She appears by your ladyship's account to have many good qualities', replied Lucy. 'Oh! a thousand,' answered Lady Williams; 'tho' I am very partial to her, and perhaps am blinded by my affection, to her real defects.'

CHAPTER THE SEVENTH

The next morning brought the three Miss Simpsons to wait on Lady Williams, who received them with the utmost politeness and introduced to their acquaintance Lucy, with whom the eldest was so much pleased that at parting she declared her sole <u>ambition</u> was to have her accompany them the next morning to Bath, whither they were going for some weeks.

'Lucy,' said Lady Williams, 'is quite at her own disposal and if she chooses to accept so kind an invitation, I hope she will not hesitate, from any motives of delicacy on my account. I know not indeed how I shall ever be able to part with her. She never was at Bath and I should think that it would be a most agreable Jaunt to her. Speak my Love,' continued she, turning to Lucy, 'what say you to accompanying these Ladies? I shall be miserable without you – t'will be a most pleasant tour to you – I hope you'll go; if you do I am sure t'will be the Death of me – pray be persuaded'—

Lucy begged leave to decline the honour of accompanying them, with many expressions of gratitude for the extream politeness of Miss Simpson in inviting her.

Miss Simpson appeared much disappointed by her refusal. Lady Williams insisted on her going – declared that she would never forgive her if she did not, and that she should never survive it if she did, and inshort used such persuasive arguments that it was at length resolved she was to go. The Miss Simpsons called for her at ten o'clock the next morning and Lady Williams had soon the satisfaction of receiving from her young freind, the pleasing intelligence of their safe arrival in Bath.

It may now be proper to return to the Hero of this Novel, the brother of Alice, of whom I beleive I have scarcely ever had occasion to speak; which may perhaps be partly oweing to his unfortunate propensity to Liquor, which so compleatly deprived him of the use of those faculties Nature had endowed him with, that he never did anything worth mentioning. His Death happened a short time after Lucy's departure and was the natural Consequence of this pernicious practice. By his decease, his sister became the sole inheritress of a very large fortune, which as it gave her fresh Hopes of rendering herself acceptable as a wife to Charles Adams could not fail of being most pleasing to her – and as the effect was Joyfull the Cause could scarcely be lamented.

Finding the violence of her attachment to him daily augment, she at length disclosed it to her Father and desired him to propose a union between them to Charles. Her father consented and set out one morning to open the affair to the young Man. Mr Johnson being a man of few words his part was soon performed and the answer he received was as follows—

'Sir, I may perhaps be expected to appear pleased at and gratefull for the offer you have made me: but let me tell you that I consider it as an affront. I look upon myself to be Sir a perfect Beauty – where would you see a finer figure or a more charming face. Then, sir I imagine my Manners and Address to be of the most polished kind; there is a certain elegance a peculiar sweetness in them that I never saw equalled and cannot describe—. Partiality aside, I am certainly more accomplished in every Language, every Science, every Art and every thing than any other person in Europe. My temper is even, my virtues innumerable, my self unparalelled. Since such Sir is my character, what do you mean by wishing me to marry your Daughter? Let me give you a short sketch of yourself and of her. I look upon you Sir to be a very good sort of Man in the main; a drunken old Dog to be sure, but that's nothing to me. Your daughter sir, is neither sufficiently beautifull, sufficiently amiable, sufficiently witty, nor sufficiently rich for me—. I expect nothing more in my wife than my wife will find in me – Perfection. These sir, are my sentiments and I honour myself for having such. One freind I have and glory in having but one—. She is at present preparing my Dinner, but if you choose to see her, she shall come and she will inform you that these have ever been my sentiments.'

Mr Johnson was satisfied; and expressing himself to be much obliged to Mr Adams for the characters he had favoured him with of himself and his Daughter, took his leave.

The unfortunate Alice on receiving from her father the sad account of the ill success his visit had been attended with, could scarcely support the disappointment – She flew to her Bottle and it was soon forgot.

CHAPTER THE EIGHTH

While these affairs were transacting at Pammydiddle, Lucy was conquering every Heart at Bath. A fortnight's residence there had nearly effaced from her remembrance the captivating form of Charles – The recollection of what her Heart had formerly suffered by his charms and her Leg by his trap, enabled her to forget him with tolerable Ease, which was what she determined to do; and for that purpose dedicated five minutes in every day to the employment of driving him from her remembrance.

Her second Letter to Lady Williams contained the

pleasing intelligence of her having accomplished her undertaking to her entire satisfaction; she mentioned in it also an offer of marriage she had received from the Duke of —— an elderly Man of noble fortune whose ill health was the chief inducement of his Journey to Bath. 'I am distressed (she continued) to know whether I mean to accept him or not. There are a thousand advantages to be derived from a marriage with the Duke, for besides those more inferior ones of Rank and Fortune it will procure me a home, which of all other things is what I most desire. Your Ladyship's kind wish of my always remaining with you, is noble and generous but I cannot think of becoming so great a burden on one I so much love and esteem. That One should receive obligations only from those we despise, is a sentiment instilled into my mind by my worthy Aunt, in my early years, and cannot in my opinion be too strictly adhered to. The excellent woman of whom I now speak, is I hear too much incensed by my imprudent departure from Wales, to receive me again—. I most earnestly wish to leave the Ladies I am now with. Miss Simpson is indeed (setting aside ambition) very amiable, but her 2^d Sister the envious and malvolent Sukey is too disagreable to live with. – I have reason to think that the admiration I have met with in the circles of the great at this Place, has raised her Hatred and Envy; for often has she threatened, and sometimes endeavoured to cut my throat. – Your Ladyship will therefore allow that I am not wrong in wishing to leave Bath, and in wishing to have a home to receive me, when I do. I shall expect with impatience your advice concerning the Duke and am your most obliged

etc etc – Lucy.'

Lady Williams sent her, her opinion on the subject in the following Manner.

'Why do you hesitate my dearest Lucy, a moment with respect to the Duke? I have enquired into his Character and find him to be an unprincipaled, illiterate Man. Never shall my Lucy be united to such a one! He has a princely fortune, which is every day encreasing. How nobly will you spend it!, what credit will you give him in the eyes of all! How much will he be respected on his Wife's account! But why my dearest Lucy, why will you not at once decide this affair by returning to me and never leaving me again? Altho' I admire your noble sentiments with respect to obligations, yet, let me beg that they may not prevent your making me happy. It will to be sure be a great expence to me, to have you always with me – I shall not be able to support it – but what is that in comparison with the happiness I shall enjoy in your society?—'twill ruin me I know—you will not therefore surely, withstand these arguments, or refuse to return to yours most affectionately—etc etc.

C. Williams'

CHAPTER THE NINTH

What might have been the effect of her Ladyship's advice, had it ever been received by Lucy, is uncertain, as it reached Bath a few Hours after she had breathed her last. She fell a sacrifice to the Envy and Malice of Sukey who jealous of her superior charms took her by poison from an admiring World at the age of seventeen.

Thus fell the amiable and lovely Lucy whose Life had been marked by no crime, and stained by no blemish but her imprudent departure from her Aunts, and whose death was sincerely lamented by every one who knew her. Among the most afflicted of her freinds were Lady Williams, Miss Johnson and the Duke; the 2 last of whom had a most sincere regard for her, more particularly Alice, who had spent a whole evening in her company and had never thought of her since. His Grace's affliction may likewise be easily accounted for, since he lost one for whom he had experienced during the last ten days, a tender affection and sincere regard. He mourned her loss with unshaken constancy for the next fortnight at the end of which time, he gratified the ambition of Caroline Simpson by raising her to the rank of a Dutchess. Thus was she at length rendered compleatly happy in the gratification of her favourite passion. Her sister the perfidious Sukey, was likewise shortly after exalted in a manner she truly deserved, and by her actions appeared to have always desired. Her barbarous Murder was discovered and in spite of every interceding freind she was speedily raised to the Gallows—. The beautifull but affected Cecilia was too sensible of her own superior charms, not to imagine that if Caroline could engage a Duke, she might without censure aspire to the affections of some Prince – and knowing that those of her native Country were cheifly engaged, she left England and I have since heard is at present the favourite Sultana of the great Mogul—.

In the mean time the inhabitants of Pammydiddle were in a state of the greatest astonishment and Wonder, a report being circulated of the intended marriage of Charles Adams. The Lady's name was still a secret. M^r and Mrs Jones imagined it to be, Miss Johnson; but <u>she</u> knew better; all <u>her</u> fears were centered in his Cook, when to the astonishment of every one, he was publicly united to Lady Williams—

Finis

Henry and Eliza

a novel

Is humbly dedicated to Miss Cooper by her obedient

Humble Servant

The Author

As Sir George and Lady Harcourt were superintending the Labours of their Haymakers, rewarding the industry of some by smiles of approbation, and punishing the idleness of others, by a cudgel, they perceived lying closely concealed beneath the thick foliage of a Haycock, a beautifull little Girl not more than 3 months old.

Touched with the enchanting Graces of her face and delighted with the infantine tho' sprightly answers she returned to their many questions, they resolved to take her home and, having no Children of their own, to educate her with care and cost.

Being good People themselves, their first and principal care was to incite in her a Love of Virtue and a Hatred of Vice, in which they so well succeeded (Eliza having a natural turn that way herself) that when she grew up, she was the delight of all who knew her.

Beloved by Lady Harcourt, adored by Sir George and admired by all the World, she lived in a continued course of uninterrupted Happiness, till she had attained her eighteenth year, when happening one day to be detected in stealing a banknote of 50£, she was turned out of doors by her inhuman Benefactors. Such a transition to one who did not possess so noble and exalted a mind as Eliza, would have been Death, but she, happy in the conscious knowledge of her own Excellence, amused herself, as she sate beneath a tree with making and singing the following Lines.

SONG.

Though misfortunes my footsteps may ever attend
   I hope I shall never have need of a Freind
as an innocent Heart I will ever preserve
   and will never from Virtue's dear boundaries swerve.

Having amused herself some hours, with this song and her own pleasing reflections, she arose and took the road to M. a small market town of which place her most intimate freind kept the red Lion.

To this freind she immediately went, to whom having recounted her late misfortune, she communicated her wish of getting into some family in the capacity of Humble Companion.

Mrs Wilson, who was the most amiable creature on earth, was no sooner acquainted with her Desire, than she sate down in the Bar and wrote the following Letter to the Dutchess of F., the woman whom of all others, she most Esteemed.

'TO THE DUTCHESS OF F.'

Receive into your Family, at my request a young woman of unexceptionable Character, who is so good as to choose your Society in preference to going to Service. Hasten, and take her from the arms of your

Sarah Wilson.

The Dutchess, whose freindship for Mrs Wilson would have carried her any lengths, was overjoyed at such an opportunity of obliging her and accordingly sate out immediately on the receipt of her letter for the red Lion, which she reached the same Evening. The Dutchess of F. was about 45 and a half; Her passions were strong, her freindships firm and her Enmities, unconquerable. She was a widow and had only one Daughter who was on the point of marriage with a young Man of considerable fortune.

The Dutchess no sooner beheld our Heroine than throwing her arms around her neck, she declared herself so much pleased with her, that she was resolved they never

more should part. Eliza was delighted with such a pro-
testation of freindship, and after taking a most affecting
leave of her dear Mrs Wilson, accompanied her grace the
next morning to her seat in Surry.

With every expression of regard did the Dutchess intro-
duce her to Lady Harriet, who was so much pleased with
her appearance that she besought her, to consider her as
her Sister, which Eliza with the greatest Condescension
promised to do.

Mr Cecil, the Lover of Lady Harriet, being often with
the family was often with Eliza. A mutual Love took place
and Cecil having declared his first, prevailed on Eliza to
consent to a private union, which was easy to be effected,
as the Dutchess's chaplain being very much in love with
Eliza himself, would they were certain do anything to
oblige her.

The Dutchess and Lady Harriet being engaged one
evening to an assembly, they took the opportunity of
their absence and were united by the enamoured
Chaplain.

When the Ladies returned, their amazement was great
at finding instead of Eliza the following Note.

'Madam
    We are married and gone.

                    Henry and Eliza Cecil.'

Her Grace as soon as she had read the letter, which
sufficiently explained the whole affair, flew into the most

violent passion and after having spent an agreable half hour, in calling them by all the shocking Names her rage could suggest to her, sent out after them 300 armed Men, with orders not to return without their Bodies, dead or alive; intending that if they should be brought to her in the latter condition to have them put to Death in some torture-like manner, after a few years Confinement.

In the mean time Cecil and Eliza continued their flight to the Continent, which they judged to be more secure than their native Land, from the dreadfull effects of the Dutchess's vengeance, which they had so much reason to apprehend.

In France they remained 3 years, during which time they became the parents of two Boys, and at the end of it Eliza became a widow without any thing to support either her or her Children. They had lived since their Marriage at the rate of 12,000£ a year, of which Mr Cecil's estate being rather less than the twentieth part, they had been able to save but a trifle, having lived to the utmost extent of their Income.

Eliza, being perfectly conscious of the derangement in their affairs, immediately on her Husband's death set sail for England, in a man of War of 55 Guns, which they had built in their more prosperous Days. But no sooner had she stepped on Shore at Dover, with a Child in each hand, than she was seized by the officers of the Dutchess, and conducted by them to a snug little Newgate of their Lady's which she had erected for the reception of her own private Prisoners.

No sooner had Eliza entered her Dungeon than the first thought which occurred to her, was how to get out of it again.

She went to the Door; but it was locked. She looked at the Window; but it was barred with iron; disappointed in both her expectations, she dispaired of effecting her Escape, when she fortunately perceived in a Corner of her Cell, a small saw and Ladder of ropes. With the saw she instantly went to work and in a few weeks had displaced every Bar but one to which she fastened the Ladder.

A difficulty then occurred which for some time, she knew not how to obviate. Her Children were too small to get down the Ladder by themselves, nor would it be possible for her to take them in her arms, when <u>she</u> did. At last she determined to fling down all her Cloathes, of which she had a large Quantity, and then having given them strict Charge not to hurt themselves, threw her Children after them. She herself with ease discended by the Ladder, at the bottom of which she had the pleasure of finding Her little boys in perfect Health and fast asleep.

Her wardrobe she now saw a fatal necessity of selling, both for the preservation of her Children and herself. With tears in her eyes, she parted with these last reliques of her former Glory, and with the money she got for them, bought others more usefull, some playthings for her Boys and a gold Watch for herself.

But scarcely was she provided with the above-mentioned necessaries, than she began to find herself rather hungry, and had reason to think, by their biting off two of her fingers, that her Children were much in the same situation.

To remedy these unavoidable misfortunes, she determined to return to her old freinds, Sir George and Lady Harcourt, whose generosity she had so often experienced and hoped to experience as often again.

She had about 40 miles to travel before she could reach their hospitable Mansion, of which having walked 30 without stopping, she found herself at the Entrance of a Town, where often in happier times, she had accompanied Sir George and Lady Harcourt to regale themselves with a cold collation at one of the Inns.

The reflections that her adventures since the last time she had partaken of these happy Junketings, afforded her, occupied her mind, for some time, as she sate on the steps at the door of a Gentleman's house. As soon as these reflections were ended, she arose and determined to take her station at the very inn, she remembered with so much delight, from the Company of which, as they went in and out, she hoped to receive some Charitable Gratuity.

She had but just taken her post at the Innyard before a Carriage drove out of it, and on turning the Corner at which she was stationed, stopped to give the Postilion an opportunity of admiring the beauty of the prospect. Eliza then advanced to the carriage and was going to request their Charity, when on fixing her Eyes on the Lady, within it, she exclaimed,

'Lady Harcourt!'

To which the lady replied,

'Eliza!'

'Yes Madam it is the wretched Eliza herself.'

Sir George, who was also in the Carriage, but too much amazed to speek, was proceeding to demand an explanation from Eliza of the Situation she was then in, when Lady Harcourt in transports of Joy, exclaimed.

'Sir George, Sir George, she is not only Eliza our adopted Daughter, but our real Child.'

'Our real Child! What Lady Harcourt, do you mean? You know you never even was with child. Explain yourself, I beseech you.'

'You must remember Sir George that when you sailed for America, you left me breeding.'

'I do, I do, go on dear Polly.'

'Four months after you were gone, I was delivered of this Girl, but dreading your just resentment at her not proving the Boy you wished, I took her to a Haycock and laid her down. A few weeks afterwards, you returned, and fortunately for me, made no enquiries on the subject. Satisfied within myself of the wellfare of my Child, I soon forgot I had one, insomuch that when, we shortly after found her in the very Haycock, I had placed her, I had no more idea of her being my own, than you had, and nothing I will venture to say would have recalled the circumstance to my remembrance, but my thus accidentally hearing her voice, which now strikes me as being the very counterpart of my own Child's.'

'The rational and convincing Account you have given of the whole affair,' said Sir George, 'leaves no doubt of her being our Daughter and as such I freely forgive the robbery she was guilty of.'

A mutual Reconciliation then took place, and Eliza, ascending the Carriage with her two Children returned to that home from which she had been absent nearly four years.

No sooner was she reinstated in her accustomed power at Harcourt Hall, than she raised an Army, with which she entirely demolished the Dutchess's Newgate, snug as it was, and by that act, gained the Blessings of thousands, and the Applause of her own Heart.

Finis

The beautifull Cassandra

*a novel in twelve Chapters dedicated
by permission to Miss Austen.*

DEDICATION.

Madam

You are a Phoenix. Your taste is refined, your Sentiments are noble, and your Virtues innumerable. Your Person is lovely, your Figure, elegant, and your Form, magestic. Your Manners are polished, your Conversation is rational and your appearance singular. If therefore the following Tale will afford one moment's amusement to you, every wish will be gratified of

> your most obedient
> humble Servant
> The Author

CHAPTER THE FIRST

Cassandra was the Daughter and the only Daughter of a celebrated Millener in Bond Street. Her father was of noble Birth, being the near relation of the Dutchess of ——'s Butler.

CHAPTER THE 2ᴰ

When Cassandra had attained her 16th year, she was lovely and amiable and chancing to fall in love with an elegant Bonnet, her Mother had just compleated bespoke by the Countess of —— she placed it on her gentle Head and walked from her Mother's shop to make her Fortune.

CHAPTER THE 3ᴰ

The first person she met, was the Viscount of —— a young Man, no less celebrated for his Accomplishments and Virtues, than for his Elegance and Beauty. She curtseyed and walked on.

CHAPTER THE 4ᵀᴴ

She then proceeded to a Pastry-cooks where she devoured six ices, refused to pay for them, knocked down the Pastry Cook and walked away.

CHAPTER THE 5ᵀᴴ

She next ascended a Hackney Coach and ordered it to Hampstead, where she was no sooner arrived than she ordered the Coachman to turn round and drive her back again.

CHAPTER THE 6ᵀᴴ

Being returned to the same spot of the same Street she had sate out from, the Coachman demanded his Pay.

CHAPTER THE 7ᵀᴴ

She searched her pockets over again and again; but every search was unsuccessfull. No money could she find. The man grew peremptory. She placed her bonnet on his head and ran away.

CHAPTER THE 8ᵀᴴ

Thro' many a street she then proceeded and met in none the least Adventure till on turning a Corner of Bloomsbury Square, she met Maria.

CHAPTER THE 9TH

Cassandra started and Maria seemed surprised; they trembled, blushed, turned pale and passed each other in a mutual silence.

CHAPTER THE 10TH

Cassandra was next accosted by her freind the Widow, who squeezing out her little Head thro' her less window, asked her how she did? Cassandra curtseyed and went on.

CHAPTER THE 11TH

A quarter of a mile brought her to her paternal roof in Bond Street from which she had now been absent nearly 7 hours.

CHAPTER THE 12TH

She entered it and was pressed to her Mother's bosom by that worthy woman. Cassandra smiled and whispered to herself 'This is a day well spent.'

Finis

Letter the third

*From A young Lady in distress'd
Circumstances to her freind*

A few days ago I was at a private Ball given by Mr Ashburnham. As my Mother never goes out she entrusted me
to the care of Lady Greville who did me the honour of
calling for me in her way and of allowing me to sit for-
wards, which is a favour about which I am very indifferent
especially as I know it is considered as confering a great
obligation on me. 'So Miss Maria' (said her Ladyship as
she saw me advancing to the door of the Carriage) 'you
seem very smart to night – <u>My</u> poor Girls will appear
quite to disadvantage by <u>you</u> – I only hope your Mother
may not have distressed herself to set <u>you</u> off. Have you
got a new Gown on?'

'Yes Ma'am,' replied I with as much indifference as I
could assume.

'Aye, and a fine one too I think—' (feeling it, as by her
permission I seated myself by her) 'I dare say it is all very
smart – But I must own, for you know I always speak my
mind, that I think it was quite a needless peice of
expence – Why could not you have worn your old striped
one? It is not my way to find fault with people because

37

they are poor, for I always think that they are more to be despised and pitied than blamed for it, especially if they cannot help it, but at the same time I must say that in my opinion your old striped Gown would have been quite fine enough for its Wearer – for to tell you the truth (I always speak my mind) I am very much afraid that one half of the people in the room will not know whether you have a Gown on or not – But I suppose you intend to make your fortune tonight—: Well, the sooner the better; and I wish you success.'

'Indeed, Ma'am, I have no such intention—'

'Who ever heard a Young Lady own that she was a Fortune-hunter?' Miss Greville laughed, but I am sure Ellen felt for me.

'Was your Mother gone to bed before you left her?' said her Ladyship—

'Dear Ma'am,' said Ellen, 'it is but nine o'clock.'

'True, Ellen, but Candles cost money, and Mrs Williams is too wise to be extravagant.'

'She was just sitting down to supper, Ma'am—'

'And what had she got for Supper?' 'I did not observe.' 'Bread and Cheese I suppose.' 'I should never wish for a better supper,' said Ellen. 'You have never any reason' replied her Mother, 'as a better is always provided for you.' Miss Greville laughed excessively, as she constantly does at her Mother's wit.

Such is the humiliating Situation in which I am forced to appear while riding in her Ladyship's Coach – I dare not be impertinent, as my Mother is always admonishing me to be humble and patient if I wish to make my way in the world. She insists on my accepting every invitation of Lady Greville, or you may be certain that I would never enter either her House, or her Coach, with the disagreable certainty I always have of being abused for my Poverty while I am in them. – When we arrived at Ashburnham, it was nearly ten o'clock, which was an hour and a half later than we were desired to be there; but Lady Greville is too fashionable (or fancies herself to be so) to be punctual. The Dancing however was not begun as they waited for Miss Greville. I had not been long in the room before I was engaged to dance by Mr Bernard, but just as we were going to stand up, he recollected that his Servant had got his white Gloves, and immediately ran out to fetch them. In the mean time the Dancing began and Lady Greville in passing to another room went exactly before me – She saw me and instantly stopping, said to me though there were several people close to us;

'Hey day, Miss Maria! What cannot you get a partner? Poor Young Lady! I am afraid your new Gown was put on for nothing. But do not despair; perhaps you may get a hop before the Evening is over.' So saying, she passed on without hearing my repeated assurance of being engaged, and leaving me very provoked at being so exposed before every one – Mr Bernard however soon returned and by coming to me the moment he entered the room, and leading me to the Dancers, my Character I hope was cleared from the imputation Lady Greville had thrown on it, in the eyes of all the old Ladies who had heard her speech. I soon forgot all my vexations in the pleasure of dancing and of having the most agreable partner in the room. As he is moreover heir to a very large Estate I could see that Lady Greville did not look very well pleased when she found who had been his Choice – She was determined to mortify me, and accordingly when we were sitting down between the dances, she came to me with <u>more</u> than her usual insulting importance attended by Miss Mason and said loud enough to be heard by half the people in the room, 'Pray, Miss Maria, in what way of business was your Grandfather? for Miss Mason and I cannot agree whether he was a Grocer or a Bookbinder.' I saw that she wanted to mortify me, and was resolved if I possibly could to prevent her seeing that her scheme succeeded. 'Neither Madam; he was a Wine Merchant.' 'Aye, I knew he was in some such low way – He broke did not he?' 'I beleive not Ma'am.' 'Did not he abscond?' 'I never heard that he did.' 'At least he died insolvent?' 'I was never told so before.' 'Why, was not your <u>Father</u> as poor as a Rat?' 'I fancy not.' 'Was not he in the King's Bench once?' 'I never saw him there.' <u>She</u> gave me <u>such</u> a look, and turned away in a great passion; while I was half delighted with myself for my impertinence, and half afraid of being thought too saucy. As Lady Greville was extremely angry with me, she took no further notice of me all the Evening, and indeed had I been in favour I should have been equally neglected, as she was got into a party of great folks and she never speaks to me when she can to any one else. Miss Greville was with her Mother's party at Supper, but Ellen preferred staying with the Bernards and me. We had a very pleasant Dance and as Lady G —— slept all the way home, I had a very comfortable ride.

The next day while we were at dinner Lady Greville's Coach stopped at the door, for that is the time of day she generally contrives it should. She sent in a message by the Servant to say that 'she should not get out but that Miss Maria must come to the Coach-door, as she wanted to speak to her, and that she must make haste and come immediately—' 'What an impertinent Message Mama!' said I—'Go Maria—' replied She – Accordingly I went and was obliged to stand there at her Ladyship's pleasure though the Wind was extremely high and very cold.

'Why I think, Miss Maria, you are not quite so smart as you were last night – But I did not come to examine your dress, but to tell you that you may dine with us the day after tomorrow – Not tomorrow, remember, do not come tomorrow, for we expect Lord and Lady Clermont and Sir Thomas Stanley's family – There will be no occasion for your being very fine for I shan't send the Carriage – If it rains you may take an umbrella—' I could hardly help laughing at hearing her give me leave to keep myself dry – 'And pray remember to be in time, for

I shan't wait – I hate my Victuals over-done – But you need not come <u>before</u> the time – How does your Mother do? She is at dinner is not she?' 'Yes, Ma'am, we were in the middle of dinner when your Ladyship came.' 'I am afraid you find it very cold, Maria,' said Ellen. 'Yes, it is an horrible East wind'—said her Mother—'I assure you I can hardly bear the window down – But you are used to be blown about the wind, Miss Maria, and that is what has made your Complexion so ruddy and coarse. You young Ladies who cannot often ride in a Carriage never mind what weather you trudge in, or how the wind shews your legs. I would not have <u>my</u> Girls stand out of doors as you do in such a day as this. But some sort of people have no feelings either of cold or Delicacy – Well, remember that we shall expect you on Thursday at 5 o'clock – You must tell your Maid to come for you at night – There will be no Moon – and you will have an horrid walk home – My Compliments to your Mother – I am afraid your dinner will be cold – Drive on—' And away she went, leaving me in a great passion with her as she always does.

Maria Williams

From a Young Lady very much in love to her Freind

My Uncle gets more stingy, my Aunt more particular, and I more in love every day. What shall we all be at this rate by the end of the year! I had this morning the happiness of receiving the following Letter from my dear Musgrove.

Sackville St: Jan^{ry} 7th

It is a month to day since I beheld my lovely Henrietta, and the sacred anniversary must and shall be kept in a manner becoming the day – by writing to her. Never shall I forget the moment when her Beauties first broke on my sight – No time as you well know can erase it from my Memory. It was at Lady Scudamore's. Happy Lady Scudamore to live within a mile of the divine Henrietta! When the lovely Creature first entered the room, Oh! what were my sensations? The sight of you was like the sight of a wonderful fine Thing. I started – I gazed at her with Admiration – She appeared every moment more Charming, and the unfortunate Musgrove became a Captive to your Charms before I had time to look about me.

Yes Madam, I had the happiness of adoring you, an unhappiness for which I cannot be too grateful. 'What,' said he to himself, 'is Musgrove allowed to die for Henrietta? Enviable Mortal! and may he pine for her who is the object of universal Admiration, who is adored by a Colonel, and toasted by a Baronet!—' Adorable Henrietta how beautiful you are! I declare you are quite divine! You are more than Mortal. You are an Angel. You are Venus herself. Inshort, Madam, you are the prettiest Girl I ever saw in my Life – and her Beauty is encreased in her Musgrove's Eyes, by permitting him to love her and allowing me to hope. And Ah! Angelic Miss Henrietta, Heaven is my Witness how ardently I do hope for the death of your villanous Uncle and his Abandoned Wife, Since my fair one will not consent to be mine till their decease has placed her in affluence above what my fortune can procure—. Though it is an improvable Estate—. Cruel Henrietta to persist in such a resolution! I am at present with my Sister where I mean to continue till my own house which tho' an excellent one is at present somewhat out of repair, is ready to receive me. Amiable princess of my Heart farewell – Of that Heart which trembles while it signs itself your most ardent Admirer

> and devoted humble Servt
>
> T. Musgrove

There is a pattern for a Love-letter Matilda! Did you ever read such a masterpeice of Writing? Such Sense,

Such Sentiment, Such purity of Thought, Such flow of Language and such unfeigned Love in one Sheet? No, never I can answer for it, since a Musgrove is not to be met with by every Girl. Oh! how I long to be with him! I intend to send him the following in answer to his Letter tomorrow.

My dearest Musgrove—. Words can not express how happy your Letter made me; I thought I should have cried for Joy, for I love you better than any body in the World. I think you the most amiable, and the handsomest Man in England, and so to be sure you are. I never read so sweet a Letter in my Life. Do write me another just like it, and tell me you are in love with me in every other line. I quite die to see you. How shall we manage to see one another? for we are so much in love that we cannot live asunder. Oh! my dear Musgrove you cannot think how impatiently I wait for the death of my Uncle and Aunt – If they will not die soon, I beleive I shall run mad, for I get more in love with you every day of my Life. How happy your Sister is to enjoy the pleasure of your Company in her house, and how happy every body in London must be because you are there. I hope you will be so kind as to write to me again soon, for I never read such sweet Letters as yours. I am, my dearest Musgrove, most truly and faithfully yours for ever and ever

Henrietta Halton

I hope he will like my answer; it is as good a one as I can write, though nothing to his; Indeed I had always heard what a dab he was at a Love-letter. I saw him you know for the first time at Lady Scudamore's – And when I saw her Ladyship afterwards she asked me how I liked her Cousin Musgrove?

'Why upon my word' said I, 'I think he is a very hand-some young Man.'

'I am glad you think so,' replied she, 'for he is distract-edly in love with you.'

'Law! Lady Scudamore,' said I, 'how can you talk so ridiculously?'

'Nay, 'tis very true,' answered She, 'I assure you, for he was in love with you from the first moment he beheld you.'

'I wish it may be true,' said I, 'for that is the only kind of love I would give a farthing for – There is some Sense in being in love at first sight.'

'Well, I give you Joy of your conquest,' replied Lady Scudamore, 'and I beleive it to have been a very complete one; I am sure it is not a contemptible one, for my Cousin is a charming young fellow, has seen a great deal of the World, and writes the best Love-letters I ever read.'

This made me very happy, and I was excessively pleased with my conquest. However I thought it was proper to give myself a few Airs – So I said to her—

'This is all very pretty, Lady Scudamore, but you know that we young Ladies who are Heiresses must not throw ourselves away upon Men who have no fortune at all.'

'My dear Miss Halton,' said She, 'I am as much convinced of that as you can be, and I do assure you that I should be the last person to encourage your marrying any one who had not some pretensions to expect a fortune with you. Mr Musgrove is so far from being poor that he has an estate of Several hundreds an year which is capable of great Improvement, and an excellent House, though at present it is not quite in repair.'

'If that is the case,' replied I, 'I have nothing more to say against him, and if as you say he is an informed young Man and can write good Love-letters, I am sure I have no reason to find fault with him for admiring me, tho' perhaps I may not marry him for all that, Lady Scudamore.'

'You are certainly under no obligation to marry him,' answered her Ladyship, 'except that which love himself will dictate to you, for if I am not greatly mistaken you are at this very moment unknown to yourself, cherishing a most tender affection for him.'

'Law, Lady Scudamore,' replied I blushing, 'how can you think of such a thing?'

'Because every look, every word betrays it,' answered She; 'Come, my dear Henrietta, consider me as a freind, and be sincere with me – Do not you prefer Mr Musgrove to any man of your acquaintance?'

'Pray do not ask me such questions, Lady Scudamore,' said I turning away my head, 'for it is not fit for me to answer them.'

'Nay my Love,' replied she, 'now you confirm my suspicions. But why, Henrietta, should you be ashamed to own a well-placed Love, or why refuse to confide in me?'

'I am not ashamed to own it;' said I taking Courage. 'I do not refuse to confide in you or blush to say that I do love your cousin Mr Musgrove, that I am sincerely attached to him, for it is no disgrace to love a handsome Man. If he were plain indeed I might have had reason to be ashamed of a passion which must have been mean since the Object would have been unworthy. But with such a figure and face, and such beautiful hair as your Cousin has, why should I blush to own that such Superior Merit has made an impression on me.'

'My sweet Girl' (said Lady Scudamore embracing me with great Affection) 'what a delicate way of thinking you have in these Matters, and what a quick discernment for one of your years! Oh! how I honour you for such Noble Sentiments!'

'Do you, Ma'am?' said I; 'You are vastly obliging. But pray, Lady Scudamore, did your Cousin himself tell you of his Affection for me? I shall like him the better if he did, for what is a Lover without a Confidante?'

'Oh! my Love' replied She, 'you were born for each other. Every word you say more deeply convinces me that your Minds are actuated by the invisible power of simpathy, for your opinions and Sentiments so exactly coincide. Nay, the colour of your Hair is not very different. Yes, my dear Girl, the poor despairing Musgrove did

reveal to me the story of his Love—. Nor was I surprised
at it – I know not how it was, but I had a kind of presen-
timent that he <u>would</u> be in love with you.'

'Well, but how did he break it to you?'

'It was not till after supper. We were sitting round the
fire together talking on indifferent subjects, though to
say the truth the Conversation was cheifly on my side, for
he was thoughtful and silent, when on a sudden he interrupted me in the midst of something I was saying, by
exclaiming in a most Theatrical tone—

"Yes I'm in love I feel it now

And Henrietta Halton has undone me—"'

'Oh! What a sweet Way' replied I, 'of declaring his
Passion! To make such a couple of charming Lines about
me! What a pity it is that they are not in rhime!'

'I am very glad you like it,' answered She; 'To be sure
there was a great deal of Taste in it. "And are you in love
with her, Cousin?" said I. "I am very sorry for it, for unexceptionable as you are in every respect, with a pretty
Estate capable of Great improvements, and an excellent
House tho' somewhat out of repair, Yet who can hope to
aspire with success to the adorable Henrietta who has had
an offer from a Colonel and been toasted by a Baronet—"'
'<u>That</u> I have—' cried I. Lady Scudamore continued. '"Ah,
dear Cousin," replied he, "I am so well convinced of the
little Chance I can have of winning her who is adored by
thousands, that I need no assurances of yours to make
me more thoroughly so. Yet surely neither you or the fair

49

Henrietta herself will deny me the exquisite Gratification of dieing for her, of falling a victim of her Charms. And when I am dead" – continued he—'

'Oh Lady Scudamore,' said I wiping my eyes, 'that such a sweet Creature should talk of dieing!'

'It is an affecting Circumstance indeed,' replied Lady Scudamore. ' "When I am dead," said he, "Let me be carried and lain at her feet, and perhaps she may not disdain to drop a pitying tear on my poor remains." '

'Dear Lady Scudamore' interrupted I, 'say no more on this affecting Subject. I cannot bear it.'

'Oh! how I admire the sweet Sensibility of your Soul, and as I would not for Worlds wound it too deeply, I will be silent.'

'Pray go on' said I. She did so.

' "And then," added he, "Ah! Cousin, imagine what my transports will be when I feel the dear precious drops trickle o'er my face! Who would not die to taste such extacy! And when I am interred, may the divine Henrietta bless some happier Youth with her affection, May he be as tenderly attached to her as the hapless Musgrove and while <u>he</u> crumbles to dust, May they live an example of Felicity in the Conjugal state!" '

'Did you ever hear any thing so pathetic? What a charming wish, to be lain at my feet when he was dead! Oh! what an exalted mind he must have to be capable of such a wish!' Lady Scudamore went on.

' "Ah! my dear Cousin," replied I to him, "Such noble

behaviour as this, must melt the heart of any Woman however obdurate it may naturally be; and could the divine Henrietta but hear your generous wishes for her happiness, all gentle as is her Mind, I have not a doubt but that she would pity your affection and endeavour to return it." "Oh! Cousin," answered he, "do not endeavour to raise my hopes by such flattering Assurances. No, I cannot hope to please this angel of a Woman, and the only thing which remains for me to do, is to die." "True Love is ever desponding," replied I, "but I, my dear Tom, will give you even greater hopes of conquering this fair one's heart, than I have yet given you, by assuring you that I watched her with the strictest attention during the whole day, and could plainly discover that she cherishes in her bosom though unknown to herself, a most tender affection for you." '

'Dear Lady Scudamore,' cried I, 'This is more than I ever knew!'

'Did not I say that it was unknown to yourself? "I did not," continued I to him, "encourage you by saying this at first, that Surprise might render the pleasure Still Greater." "No, Cousin," replied he in a languid voice, "nothing will convince me that I can have touched the heart of Henrietta Halton, and if you are deceived yourself, do not attempt deceiving me." Inshort my Love it was the work of some hours for me to persuade the poor despairing Youth that you had really a preference for him; but when at last he could no longer deny the force of my arguments, or discredit what I told him, his transports, his Raptures, his Extacies are beyond my power to describe.'

'Oh! the dear Creature,' cried I, 'how passionately he loves me! But, dear Lady Scudamore, did you tell him that I was totally dependant on my Uncle and Aunt?'

'Yes, I told him every thing.'

'And what did he say?'

'He exclaimed with virulence against Uncles and Aunts; Accused the Laws of England for allowing them to possess their Estates when wanted by their Nephews or Neices, and wished <u>he</u> were in the House of Commons, that he might reform the Legislature, and rectify all its abuses.'

'Oh! the sweet Man! What a spirit he has!' said I.

'He could not flatter himself, he added, that the adorable Henrietta would condescend for his Sake to resign those Luxuries and that Splendor to which She had been used, and accept only in exchange the Comforts and Elegancies which his limited Income could afford her, even supposing that his house were in Readiness to receive her. I told him that it could not be expected that she would; it would be doing her an injustice to suppose her capable of giving up the power she now possesses and so nobly uses of doing such extensive Good to the poorer part of her fellow Creatures, merely for the gratification of you and herself.'

'To be sure,' said I, 'I <u>am</u> very Charitable every now and then. And what did Mr Musgrove say to this?'

'He replied that he was under a melancholy Necessity of owning the truth of what I said, and therefore if he should be the happy Creature destined to be the Husband of the Beautiful Henrietta he must bring himself to wait, however impatiently, for the fortunate day, when she might be freed from the power of worthless Relations and able to bestow herself on him.'

What a noble Creature he is! Oh! Matilda what a fortunate one <u>I am</u>, who am to be his Wife! My Aunt is calling to me to come and make the pies. So adeiu my dear freind,

and beleive me yours etc. – H. Halton

Finis

*A Letter from a Young Lady, whose feelings
being too Strong for her Judgement led her
into the commission of Errors which
her Heart disapproved*

Many have been the cares and vicissitudes of my past life,
my beloved Ellinor, and the only consolation I feel for
their bitterness is that on a close examination of my conduct, I am convinced that I have strictly deserved them.
I murdered my father at a very early period of my Life, I
have since murdered my Mother, and I am now going to
murder my Sister. I have changed my religion so often
that at present I have not an idea of any left. I have been
a perjured witness in every public tryal for these last
twelve Years, and I have forged my own Will. In short
there is scarcely a crime that I have not committed – But
I am now going to reform. Colonel Martin of the Horse
guards has paid his Addresses to me, and we are to be
married in a few days. As there is something singular in
our Courtship, I will give you an account of it. Colonel
Martin is the second son of the late Sir John Martin who
died immensely rich, but bequeathing only one hundred
thousand pound apiece to his three younger Children,

left the bulk of his fortune, about eight Million to the present Sir Thomas. Upon his small pittance the Colonel lived tolerably contented for nearly four months when he took it into his head to determine on getting the whole of his eldest Brother's Estate. A new will was forged and the Colonel produced it in Court – but nobody would swear to it's being the right Will except himself, and he had sworn so much that Nobody beleived him. At that moment I happened to be passing by the door of the Court, and was beckoned in by the Judge who told the Colonel that I was a Lady ready to witness anything for the cause of Justice, and advised him to apply to me. In short the Affair was soon adjusted. The Colonel and I swore to its' being the right will, and Sir Thomas has been obliged to resign all his illgotten Wealth. The Colonel in gratitude waited on me the next day with an offer of his hand—. I am now going to murder my Sister.

Yours Ever,

Anna Parker